FLIGHT OF THE
FALCON

CREATION ADVENTURE SERIES

FLIGHT OF THE

FALCON

The Thrilling Adventures of Colonel Jim Irwin

PAUL THOMSEN

INSTITUTE FOR CREATION RESEARCH
SANTEE, CALIFORNIA

Unless otherwise noted, all Scripture quotations are from the New King James Version of the Bible, © 1979, 1980, 1982, 1984 by Thomas Nelson, Inc., Nashville, Tennessee and are used by permission.

Illustrations by Brian Thompson

Institute for Creation Research
P.O. Box 2667
El Cajon, California 92021
1 (800) 628-7640

Library of Congress Cataloging in Publication Data

Thomsen, Paul M., 1938—
    The flight of the falcon: the thrilling adventures of astronaut Jim Irwin/Paul Thomsen.—2nd ed.
        p. cm.—(Creation adventure series)
    ISBN 0-932766-45-5
    1. Irwin, James B. (James Benson) 2. Astronauts—United States—Biography. I. Title.
TL789.85.I78T46 1991
629.45'0092—d2

[B]

97-070391
CIP

To my kids,
all seven of them!

CHAPTER 1

The lone climber calculated each step down with precision, placing his heavy-duty climbing boots into the best niches around the jagged rocks. His right hand wedged an ice pick into the steeply graded ledge, slowing his descent, while his left arm reached out into space for balance. Each crunch of his boots sent a miniavalanche of stones tumbling down the sharp precipice. With a crack they bounded high, then shot down a steep, four-hundred-meter snow slope, shooting geysers of white snow and ice crystals out into the blue sky far below the descending climber.

Reaching the edge of the snow-covered slope, the fatigued man halted, his chest heaving for precious air—rare at fifteen thousand feet. The icy wind whipped bits of sweat off the five-day stubble of whiskers on his chin as he loosened the straps on his forty-pound backpack, squatted down, and leaned back against it, digging his heels into the leading edge of the snow for a brace.

Hunkering down lower against the biting wind, he pulled down his dark goggles. Immediately tears poured from his squinting eyes. As he adjusted to the brilliance, a spectacular panorama played out before him. To his left lay Iran and Iraq—straight out, the plains of Turkey—over his right shoulder, Russia—and out there, just over the horizon, Israel. He thought how privileged he was to breathe in the same air, sit on the same rocks, and view the same splendor that Noah had some four thousand years earlier. It was Noah's mighty ship that had come to rest on this mountain after floating for five months on water that had completely covered the earth. It was that Ark—the lost Ark—that the climber and his team were seeking.

Two hours before, only a thousand feet shy of the summit, Colonel Irwin had ordered his men to continue on; he would return alone to base camp at the fourteen-thousand-foot mark.

*The lone climber calculated
each step down with precision.*

It was only on his direct order as expedition leader that the final assault team reluctantly turned and continued the trek to the summit.

His lungs sucked in huge gulps of thin air as his dark brown eyes spotted the sun reflecting off the golden wings of a falcon. The big predator extended his talons and with folded wings dove through a streak of white clouds into the Ahora Gorge thousands of feet below. The majestic view and diving bird reminded him of his test pilot days, flying high above his native California for the United States Air Force. Back then, he was one of a very select few chosen to be part of a top secret program designed as the first phase for gaining knowledge of how man and equipment would operate in the weightless condition and high altitudes of near space. It took a special breed of men to tread the hostile world of the unknown—courageous men not afraid to walk the razor's edge of life and death, not afraid to pierce the edge of space and pave the way for the ultimate objective—putting a man on the moon. Back then, Captain Irwin had earned the test pilot's enviable title, Top Gun.

*. . . the sun reflecting off
the golden wings of a falcon.*

As the pounding in the climber's heart slowly subsided, the only sound breaking the silence was an occasional shrill whistle as an icy gust whipped around the tubing on his backpack. His eyes shifted to the snow ledge that dropped sharply beneath, the next major traverse in his descent. He calculated the descent down the treacherous drop-off. One slip and it would be a mighty fast ride to the rocks below, but the maneuver didn't scare him; rather, he looked to the challenge with excited anticipation. He'd been in that "hairy" position before when life hung by a fraction—a millisecond—back in his test pilot days flying on the razor's edge in that aircraft of aircrafts, the F-104 *Starfighter*.

What an incredible plane—fifty-four feet of slick aluminum from its needle nose to the tip of its high-backed tail. The short, slightly swept back wings were so sharp at the leading edge that protective covers were put on to keep ground crews in the hangar from accidentally slicing themselves open if they should brush up against them—all this wrapped around a powerful J-79 engine that flat out, with afterburner, would blast the plane past Mach two—thirteen hundred miles per hour.

His heaving chest began to subside as he gazed out over the clear sky from high on his lone perch. Checking his watch, he set the timer, allowing himself exactly seven more minutes of recoup time—any longer and he knew his muscles would stiffen and cramp at this altitude. Nestling down a bit further, he allowed his mind to drift back again to that one particular day at Edwards Air Force Base—the day of the "Zoom" flight. It was a day just like this, where a guy could see forever. While he looked out over the panorama, he thought back to that one special flight.

ᛒᛒ ᛒᛒ ᛒᛒ

He pictured himself in his tight, form-fitting pressure suit and dark-visored helmet as he climbed to the cockpit of the F-104 *Starfighter*. With one foot in, he glanced at the American flag above the call sign "BY" (Bravo-Yankee) proudly painted on the plane's tail; a smart salute, and he slipped into the seat. He inserted hooks, called "spurs," on the back of his flight boots into catches at the base of the seat, then pushed his feet to the rudder pedals pulling out cables attached to his spurs from under the base of the seat. Then, buckling his shoulder harness and parachute "D" ring, he reached down and pulled the pins for the ejection seat, making it "hot"—ready for action. The canopy came down on the taxi to the active runway; and with tower clearance he throttled up. Halfway down the twelve-thousand-foot runway he hit two hundred knots and rotated the needle nose up. The thundering jet rose quickly.

"Departure Control, this is *Starfighter* Bravo-Yankee with you out of five thousand."

"Roger, Bravo-Yankee, you're cleared to fifty-five thousand. Maintain a heading of two-niner-five."

Leveling off at fifty-five thousand, he spotted Tommy Bell in his chase plane coming up and closing at the three o'clock position. The chase plane would "ride shotgun," keeping an eye on Bravo-Yankee as he executed the "Zoom" flight.

"Bravo-Yankee, we have you locked on radar and cleared to initiate power-up," crackled Control ten miles below.

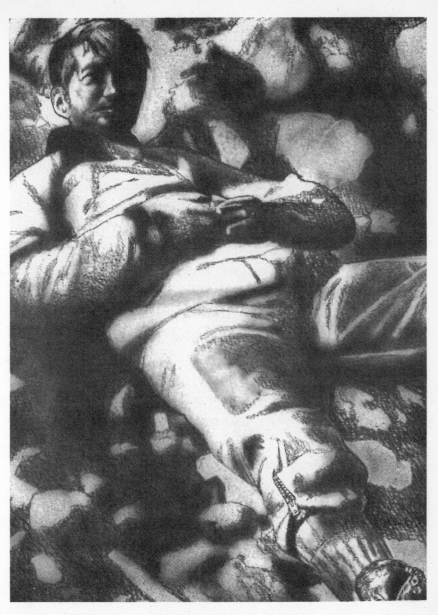

Nestling down a bit further,
he allowed his mind to drift . . .

"Roger, Control, I'll go sonic now." With his right hand he gave a "thumbs up" to Bell cruising off his starboard wingtip, then pushed the throttle past the detent position to full power. Raw kerosene poured into the second set of burners in the huge engine; the nozzle at the exhaust opened wide as a twenty-foot orange flame blasted the plane past Mach one, the speed of sound. The air wall in front of the plane collapsed around the needle nose, sending a sonic boom thundering across the desert sand twenty miles behind the now sonic jet. Captain Irwin's eyes scanned the instruments; the airspeed indicator went past seven hundred knots. As his helmet and body were sucked back into the seat by the fired-up afterburner, he passed Mach two with barely a shudder. Easing the yoke forward an inch, he put the plane in a slightly downward altitude, eking out that last bit of speed. He was now flying faster than a bullet coming out of a rifle.

"Bravo-Yankee, radar has you accelerating through 1,380 miles per hour at 54,800 feet. Commence 'Zoom' at your discretion."

"Roger, Control. See ya' on the way back down, Tommy."

"Roger, Bravo-Yankee. I'll keep watch from down here."

Every fiber of his body was concentrated on the machine and its instruments. Even though the outside air temperature was minus ninety degrees Fahrenheit, the leading edge of the jet's razor-sharp wings had turned white-hot from air friction and the aluminum-skin alloy had begun to expand under the extreme heat and pressure. With the delicate touch of a surgeon, he eased back on the yoke, lifting the needle nose ever so gradually. His eyes were glued unblinkingly on the instruments, every bit of his being anticipating each small move Bravo-Yankee would have to endure through the "Zoom." Now pilot and plane had melded into one maxed-out unit, operating at their combined limits in a singular, supersonic ballet of nerves, metal, and fire.

"Have you going through sixty-five thousand and climbing rapidly."

"Roger."

The tight-fitting pressure suit automatically inflated. As the suit stiffened, the controls became a bit more difficult to operate; but without it, he would lose consciousness within seconds in the near-zero pressure of high altitude. Firmly, he pulled back on the stick, pointing the needle nose toward the blackness of space; the jet roared nearly straight up at full power.

"Going through seventy-five thousand and shutting down the engine." With his left hand, he flipped off the ignition switch and pulled the throttle back to the neutral detent. Instantly, the twenty-foot flame went out and the red-hot exhaust nozzle closed in. If left running in the rare atmosphere above seventy-five thousand, the powerful engine would become oxygen starved and the metal would "freeze," or even worse, explode. Having completed his "slingshot" phase, he was in a non-powered climb. Scanning the instruments, he watched the airspeed indicator begin to drop while the altimeter continued to climb through eighty-five thousand. From here on it was no-man's-land—what was about to happen to pilot and machine was unknown. He could only react to whatever contingency transpired when the limit of the two had been reached.

"Passing ninety-thousand, decelerating rapidly." A tense controller's voice rang amazingly

*Firmly, he pulled back on the stick, pointing
the needle nose toward the blackness of space.*

clear in the helmet of the now completely silent cockpit.

"Roger, my airspeed's under three hundred knots—I'm nearly weightless. The controls are operating okay—got rudder, aileron; speed at two hundred knots. I'm reading ninety-five thousand. Suit is stiff, but I can maneuver effectively."

"Bravo-Yankee, begin descent at your discretion."

"Roger, Control, I think I can still get a few more feet under us." *Come on, Yankee, give me another thousand—stretch for it!* Facing literally straight up, the blackness of space filled the front windscreen; to the left, the curvature of the earth was visible.

"Remember, the F-104 cannot go into a flat spin—it is totally impossible." The crucial words of his flight instructor about the most dangerous situation a test pilot could encounter, rang in Captain Irwin's ears as his eyes fixed on the airspeed indicator that had suddenly dropped to the red zone, indicating stall speed. Pushing the control stick forward, he watched the nose drop slightly, then stop. He pushed more. Nothing. The nose wouldn't drop. Tension gripped and riveted him flat against the cockpit seat. For an instant, plane and pilot hung weightless on the fringes of space nearly twenty miles straight up. Slowly at first, then faster, the twenty-thousand-pound jet started to fall tail first. Now he jammed the yoke full forward—still the nose wouldn't come down. In the near nothingness of the upper atmosphere, the craft started to plummet.

"Control, I've got a problem up here."

"Roger, Bravo-Yankee, we have you dropping through eighty-five thousand and accelerating rapidly. Chase Plane One, do you have a visual on Bravo-Yankee?"

"Affirmative," radioed Bell from the chase plane, looking up at the tiny silver dot forty thousand feet above him.

Captain Irwin pulled the yoke hard right—nothing. The thin air wasn't passing over the control mechanisms, and now the plane was falling like a rock, totally out of control. It absolutely couldn't happen, but it had! He was in a pilot's most disastrous situation. "I've got flat spin up here." Captain Irwin's voice was terse.

"Roger, Bravo-Yankee, we have you dropping through seventy-five thousand and accelerating faster."

Fighting the controls, Captain Irwin didn't answer. As the nose began to spin more rapidly, the earth flashed by his windscreen in dizzying circles while the altimeter spun downward past seventy thousand. At sixty-five thousand, he managed to raise a hand and hit the ignition switch, then push the throttle to the start position; the engine caught—fire leaped from the rear. His pressure suit deflated as cabin pressure built. Despite the fired-up engine, the plane continued its spinning plummet; without air passing over the upper surface of wings and tail, the pilot had no control.

"Base, this is Chase One. He's got the engine started, but he's still in a flat spin. He just shot by me like a fire-spitting rock. Jim, if you can read me, you better start thinkin' of ejecting."

The controller added, "Bravo-Yankee, we estimate less than sixty seconds to impact."

Captain Irwin's mind whirled through the ejection procedure. Grab the eject ring between

"He just shot by me like a fire-spitting rock."

the legs with both hands and yank up hard to the gut. The initial charge snaps the cables and feet back against the seat. The canopy blows off, head snaps back against the headrest. The arm-restraint webbing snaps around, pinning arms in so they don't tear off going out. Seat and pilot fire straight up, a rocket ignites blasting pilot and seat past the high tail. A guillotine cuts the foot cables and seat harness, and the pilot is blown away from the seat—all that in less than one second.

"Going through forty thousand, Captain Irwin," shouted the controller.

"Jim, bail out now, don't wait. Get outta there!" yelled Bell as he peeled off to follow the fire-spitting jet that was plummeting in a death spin toward impact.

Inside the cockpit, sweat ran down the pilot's oxygen mask. He whispered a gut-level prayer, "Lord, help!" His eyes flashed to the altimeter, down past twenty thousand; fifteen. *It's too late to eject—fly or die.* Intuitively, his hand grabbed the flap control. He pushed it down to the takeoff setting—fifteen degree flaps. The plane shuddered, the nose dipped slightly, stopped, then dipped again. "Come on, get down," he shouted through gritting teeth. The *Starfighter's* needle nose dipped again. "Down! Down, you can do it. Now, Yankee, now!" As the needle nose pointed down, precious air built up over the wings and airframe. His rudder came alive, then the ailerons and elevator on its high-backed tail. The windshield filled with spinning desert sand. Desperately, he again slammed his rudder pedal down. With the control mechanisms working, the spin stopped; quickly, he leveled the wings while pulling back on the yoke. The plane began to pull out of the dive.

"Come on, now. Up, up!" Irwin's eyes glued on the fast-approaching ground. He could see cactus; rocks. Clenching his teeth, he pulled back hard on the yoke. He sank into his seat; the short wings shuddered. Plane and pilot agonized under the immense g-force pressure of the pullout. At less than three thousand feet, he grabbed full control; and with an ear-shattering sonic blast, the jet bottomed out, roaring over the hot desert sand. He looked up. Dead ahead was the airport. "Thank you, Lord—thank you." Making his break, he dropped the gear and landed in one smooth motion. Pulling off at the first taxiway, he braked to a stop.

"I don't see a chute—I've got no chute. He must have gone in," yelled Bell from the chase plane.

Smiling inside his sweat-dripping oxygen mask, Captain Irwin pushed on his mike button. "Chase One, Bravo-Yankee didn't go in. I'm back at the ranch, Tommy. Come on home, partner."

ଏ ଏ ଏ

Sitting on his perch high atop the south face of Mount Ararat, the ex-test pilot/now mountain climber shook his head, clearing his mind of memories. Then he picked up a fist-sized rock, flipped it out a few feet, and watched it kick up snow as it bounded down the steep snow ledge, smashing into the boulders hundreds of feet below.

CHAPTER 2

A grin crossed his cracked lips as he recalled that day; "I pulled that one out. By comparison, this little jaunt down the ice field will be a piece of cake." Standing, he put his hands on his hips and arched his aching back, stretching muscles sore from five days on the mountain. Just as the timer on his watch beeped, he heard a slight crack behind and up. Sensing danger, he tensed. A rush of air and a mighty "Thud!"—the air burst out of his lungs, then all went white as his face smacked snow. Down the drop-off he skidded face first, arms flailing. Blue sky flashed as he somersaulted, twisting sideways, more white snow tearing at his face, black rocks, then a ripping sound as metal, fabric, and flesh twisted and tore apart. The world became a blur of sky, snow, and falling rocks as he tumbled, spun, and skidded down the sheer ice field toward the rocks beneath. With a sickening crunch of flesh on stone, all went black.

The roar of the avalanche echoed across the gorge and faded. Then the silence closed in, punctuated only by the muted flapping from the torn jacket on the climber's arm that hung over a boulder.

The afternoon wind whipped snow down the drop-off, gradually filling the gouges made by falling rocks and climber. By midafternoon all traces of the disaster were covered; not even the red streaks of frozen blood showed through.

Close to the summit the assault team had heard a distant rumble. It drew only a momentary glance back from one climber. Through the week they'd become accustomed to the sound of potential disaster; they had heard hundreds of avalanches echoing through the gorges. Their target now was the summit, then with luck, back to base camp before dark.

As the huge, burnt umber sun settled behind the western ramparts, the wind died and no

Blue sky flashed as he somersaulted. . . .

longer whipped the torn jacket on the arm draped over the boulder. Slowly, blood-caked fingers flexed, then the arm slid down, the hand moving to a battered face that lay in the recesses of volcanic rock. Fumbling, Colonel Irwin began his damage report. He could see with his left eye, but the right was badly swollen with a deep gash over it. His groping fingers moved to his pounding head, gently tracing the blood-clotted gash in his skull, then dropped to his swollen, cut lips, counting broken and missing teeth—at five he quit. Raising his arm, he looked at his shattered watch. Then, propping on an elbow, he hesitantly raised his head above the rocks, squinting with his good eye for the sun. "It's setting—that means I've been here for at least four hours. I've got to get outta here and make base camp or I'm stuck here for the night."

Slowly gathering himself, he rolled over and got to his hands and knees. Putting his hands to the boulder, he pulled himself up as thick blood dripped to the rock from his gashed nose. Half standing, he pushed back, rocked, then stood steady. Having felt no great pain, he hesitantly took a step. A searing bolt of pain and his ankle gave way, dropping him back heavily against the boulder. Resting his head flat against the rock, he gasped for air as his head spun dizzily. The hand in front of his good eye began to shiver in the cold of early evening. "My backpack—it's still on, thank God."

He wedged his thumb under the strap holding his backpack, then pushed the release buckle while twisting his back to the boulder. Sliding the other strap off his shoulder, the pack dropped to his feet. Grimacing, he slid down the boulder and with effort pulled out the sleeping bag. Crawling in, he then pulled the soft down cover over his body, tucking it under his chin. His body began to shake as chills ran up and down his spine; with each breath, spasms wracked across his ribs as his chest heaved, gasping for air. For an hour he lay enduring the agony. Then, as darkness replaced the golden sunset alpenglow, his body rebuilt heat inside the down sleeping bag and the tremors subsided. Strangely, he felt no pain as his head cleared. He prayed, "Lord, I commit my care to You. I know I'm helpless on this mountain tonight like a lost sheep. You are my shepherd. Give me comfort, O Lord. If it be in *Your* will, may I live." His clasped hands stuck with semi-dried blood. He pried them apart and slid the sleeping-bag cocoon over his head. Closing his eyes, he allowed his mind to drift. *I haven't always been in His will, but He has never forsaken me. He has taken me through the agony of helplessness. I've been in this position before—broken, battered—and my God has always been with me.*

His mind slid in and out of consciousness. *I must stay awake . . . if the assault team passes, I must cry for help . . . don't sleep now . . . think, think how the Lord carried you through and gave you that will to overcome; the will to live, to live for Him. When was that? Fifteen years ago! Seems like yesterday when I went through that plane crash and that test of faith. What was it for? Perhaps it was for now—to call upon that remembrance for strength, His strength.* Colonel Irwin thought back to those harrowing days of the crash.

℠ ℠ ℠

"Dr. John Forrest to the emergency room." The call went out over the public address system at March Air Force Hospital again—this time with urgency. "Dr. Forrest to the emergency room, STAT!"

As Dr. Forrest walked rapidly to the ER, a corpsman caught up. "It's a couple of pilots from Edwards, crashed in a light plane—one of them is in the aerospace school."

"A future astronaut?" queried Dr. Forrest, raising his eyebrows.

"Guess so; a Captain Irwin. They really had a tough time getting him over here. I understand he was thrashing so hard that he tore open the belts on the stretcher. The paramedics had to literally tie him down with rope; even then, he kept screaming, calling his baby daughter's name. It was only when his wife came rushing up and gently talked to him that he calmed down. She stood right by him through the screaming and the whole thing."

With long strides, they entered the trauma bay; Dr. Forrest saw his patient stretched out on the table. The oral surgeons were already working on his horribly crushed jaw and face. Turning, he addressed an X ray technician, "You guys got pictures of his limbs yet?" The technician assisting the oral surgeons nodded to the wall viewer. Dr. Forrest pushed up his glasses and looked at the X rays, revealing fractures in both legs. The right leg was the worst. The lower tibia bone had torn through the skin on the underside of his leg and was sticking out six inches.

As the assisting doctor and nurses prepped the pilot for surgery, Dr. Forrest took a close look at the jagged white bone protruding from the pilot's massively swollen leg. The skin on the top of the leg was so taut from the swelling that it had developed pressure cracks. Dr. Forrest felt his ankle for a pulse, indicating blood flow to the foot. There was none; the toes were turning blue. Stepping up, he looked squarely into the pilot's eyes. "Captain Irwin, besides your badly fractured jaw, you've got two broken legs; the right one is particularly serious. The swelling has constricted the vessels carrying blood to your foot. If we don't operate and relieve the pressure, there is a high risk of losing your foot. I suggest we operate immediately. Can you understand?" The dazed pilot gave a slight nod of approval.

In the operating room, Dr. Forrest searched the fractured bone and punctured area to pick out any bits of clothing or grit. Then, taking a large-bulbed syringe filled with antiseptic fluid, he squirted the protruding bone, irrigating it thoroughly. Cutting the skin and muscle back away from the underside of the leg, he took hold of the splintered bone end and pushed it back under the skin, fitting it to the other bone. The splintered pieces fit together, the shards of each end wedging into their respective places. "Like splicing a broken broom handle together," he said grimly through his green mask to the wide-eyed corpsman.

After making his internal sutures, he closed the wound with outside stitches. Reaching down, his blood-flecked hand again groped the lower ankle for a pulse. He gave the operating team a terse, one-word report, "None." The eyes of his surgical nurse darted from above her mask to the drops of blood that were oozing out of pressure cracks on the swollen upper side of the leg.

"We've got to get rid of that pressure quick. I'm going to open the anterior compartment." While keeping his eyes locked on the leg, he stretched out his hand. "Number 10 scalpel." The surgical nurse smartly slapped the

instrument into the surgeon's hand. Beginning just beneath the knee, he punctured,
then drew the razor-sharp instrument down
the shin, cutting a half-inch deep through the
drum-tight skin, stopping at the ankle. With
the skin parted in a twenty-inch slit, the facia
package containing the big upper-side
muscles was revealed, looking like a swollen
sausage in its casing. Again, he moved the
scalpel delicately, cutting open the thin
membrane of the facia package from knee to
ankle. As he drew the knife down, raw
muscle bulged out of the slit like rising bread.

"Wire."

The nurse handed the doctor a stainless steel
wire strip neatly cut to an eight-inch length.
Poking the wire through the skin on one side of
the wound, he drew it loosely over the exposed
muscle, then poked it through the skin on the
other side, leaving the two ends sticking up. Five
times he repeated the process with separate wires,
making a series of cross-muscle skin connections
leaving their ends pointing up. Taking the first set
of wire ends, he twisted them together once with
his hands. "Pliers." Using the pliers, he twisted the
ends again, drawing the wire connecting the skin

across the open wound to a firm position. He repeated the process, drawing the wires firm like a series of bread "twisties." Having completed the procedure, he stepped back, waited a minute, then once again felt the ankle for a pulse. All eyes of the surgical team focused on his hand. If there was no pulse now that the pressure had been released, the foot would have to come off, and that would be the end of a life's dream for this future astronaut. Feeling nothing, he moved his fingers slightly, his eyes and bloodstained hand searching. Then out loud, "I got one . . ." Then nothing. "Wait, got another—two, three, four. There we go, nice and steady." His eyes shot up to the team. "He's gonna keep it!" Smiles broke out under masks as they watched the pilot's toes gradually turn from blue to a robust pink. After the leg cast was applied, a window was cut in the top to reveal the wires and open wound.

Later, when Jim's wife Mary arrived at the hospital, Dr. Forrest had a talk with her. "He's mighty lucky to be alive. He almost lost his right foot. The oral surgeons have wired his jaw back together. When they periodically take him back to the operating room to do reconstruction work on his face, I'll open the

window in his right leg cast and give a twist
to the wires, drawing the skin gradually back
over the open wound. I suspect it'll take
months for us to pull the skin back and close
the wound. I understand you stood by him
through the tough part after the crash. That
took a lot of courage and strength, and it will
take a great deal more strength, Mrs. Irwin,
for that was just the beginning. The recovery
is going to be long and very, very
painful—for both of you."

Looking toward the intensive care unit,
Mary Irwin said, "My husband and I have
been through much pain and fear together.
As a test pilot's wife, I have lived with the fear
of a crash every time he left the house in the
morning. I know this fear haunted the inner
recesses of Jim's mind also. On one occasion
he awoke in the middle of the night thrashing
and screaming about a crash. His pajamas
were soaked with sweat. We just hung on to
each other, and I prayed until he calmed
down. I have prayed daily for God to give the
children and me strength if this should ever
happen. And now . . ." Speaking softly, yet
with conviction, she raised her eyes to his,

"And now that it's come upon us, well, I just have to believe God let it happen for a reason; and He'll carry us through the fire."

Dr. Forrest looked at this tender lady. Then, with eyes filled with admiration and compassion, he said, "Your faith is indeed inspiring to us all."

As the days passed, Captain Irwin was repeatedly brought into the operating room where oral surgeons worked on restoring his shattered teeth and cracked jaw. On these occasions, Dr. Forrest would open the window on his cast, check the swelling, and then as it gradually subsided, twist and tighten the wires, pulling the skin back over the open wound. Mary and the children moved into a house trailer near the hospital. Her days were spent caring for her husband, standing strong for the kids, and praying over her broken pilot. Gradually, as his senses returned, so did the excruciating pain and comprehension of reality.

He had been the top test pilot in America, chosen from the Top Guns to be one of the privileged few to enter aerospace training. He was well on the way to the very pinnacle of success, and then the next instant, this—a shattered, broken hulk.

In the dead of one hot night, he lay in searing pain. His bowels ached. He couldn't even reach over to push the call button for the nurse. He tried to call out, but nothing came through the wires on his jaw. It was a total nightmare. Alone, in pain, and in the sweat-soaked blackness of the room, he was at the bottom; the very pit of black depression encompassed him. He thought, *Why me, Lord, why me?*

Over the next three-and-a-half months, the pilot had fifteen procedures to rework his face and tighten the skin over the wound on his leg. Late one sultry evening, Dr. Forrest sat in his office drumming his fingers on the desktop while he contemplated his patient. *The wounds were healing, but the mind and will weren't. What was it that would do it? This kinda guy lives for the challenge—wait, that's it! I'll take a chance.* Kicking his chair back, he rose and briskly walked down the dark corridor. Entering the dimly lit room, he could see the test pilot was awake, staring at the ceiling. Stopping at bedside, Dr. Forrest looked at the leg, "It's healing incredibly well." His scan continued past the wired jaw, then their eyes met and locked. "I'll make you a deal, Captain. *If*—I repeat *if*—you can raise your leg, cast and all, off the bed five times, I'll let you go home. I'll be back tomorrow and see how you're doing."

That was it, what he needed; the challenge had been hurled. That night he pushed off the sheet covering him, turned on the bed lamp, and put his arms flat on either side, palms down, bracing himself for the leg lift. Straining, he lifted against the dead weight of the full hip cast. The wires dug and pulled at his skin under the plaster, and pain forced him back. Grimacing behind his wired jaw, once more he strained; the leg shook. Shooting a glance down, he saw his toes rise slightly. Relaxing, he still wasn't sure he had done it. One more time. Pulling his head back and arching, he strained with all his might. "Lord, give me strength now! Please, dear Lord." Then, glancing down again, he saw the giant white cast shake, rise an inch, two, then three. He had done it. He was airborne! As sweat poured off his forehead, he lowered the leg to the sheets. "Thank You, Lord, thank You."

The next morning a laughing Dr. Forrest had to stop his patient at twenty leg lifts. "Okay, okay, hang on there, pilot. You've soloed, let's not go through the sound barrier just yet. I'll clear you to get outta here."

Later that night, Captain Irwin had time for reflection. *Why me?* It became crystal clear. Up to the crash, he had focused his total being on himself, *on me*—in one word, pride. He needed to be broken and to trust the Lord to carry him forward, not his own strength and power. With tears in his eyes, he confessed to Jesus his sin of pride and asked forgiveness. Then as fullness of heart and a redirected faith enveloped him, he knew His Lord had forgiven him. That evening, the burning desire was once again kindled—to fly, to reach for the moon; better yet, to walk on the moon! This time it would not be *my* will be done, but rather *Thy* will be done.

80 80 80

Recalling those days and their lessons gave a surge of God-strength to the wounded, bleeding climber as he lay in the recesses of rock high on the darkening ridges of Mount Ararat.

CHAPTER 3

The fallen climber awoke from his half sleep with a jerk as something tugged at his head. Reaching back in the darkness, his hand discovered the gash in his skull had reopened; blood had clotted his hair to a rock. Wincing, he pried himself loose. It was a painful reminder that he was alone, seriously wounded, and still on the rugged slopes of Mount Ararat. The night was getting bitter cold. Still inside his sleeping bag, he slowly rolled to his back, put the good hand behind his head and eased back against the rocks, looking face up at the star-studded sky. Millions of them blanketed the night forming a jeweled background as the full moon began to rise over the eastern ridges. "Ah, my old friend—the moon—you

who were created by God, you who have
been the focus of my life, once more we meet.
We go back a long way together. Let's see,
the first time was way back in Pennsylvania. I
must have been—what? I guess about
ten-years-old. . . ." Tense muscles relaxed as
he remembered his youth.

ဆ   ဆ   ဆ

"Jimmy, your dad and I have decided we'll
let you have your plane ride. Heaven knows
why, but you certainly have pestered us
enough for it." The words from his mom sent a
shiver of expectation down the young lad's
back. "They're giving rides out by the old
property, and we've saved just enough for you
to make one flight. Your dad and I have never
been in an airplane, but I can remember back
when your grandpa let me have my first ride
in an automobile—he called it a horseless
carriage, said they'd never get him in one of
those contraptions. Well, anyway, now it's
airplanes. Lord knows what's next."

The young lad's nose was plastered to the
window as the plane rumbled down the

*The young lad's nose was plastered to the window
as the plane rumbled down the runway.*

runway and became airborne on the second bounce. The earth dropped below; their auto turned into a tiny red speck. Then as they went up through the low, puffy clouds, the moon appeared, full and white against the deep blue sky.

"Mama, we got over the clouds, and I saw the moon. Dad, I felt I could reach out and touch it! It was magnificent. Someday, I'm going to walk on the moon, just you wait and see!" rattled the wide-eyed young lad, excitedly stomping his foot on the ground.

"Just you calm down now, Jim," said a stern Father Irwin. "I'm glad you had your ride, but enough of this foolish talk about walking on the moon. No man has ever been up there, no man ever will. That stuff is only in comic books!" Walking hand in hand with his dad back to the car, young Jim glanced back over his shoulder as the pilot revved up the engine for another takeoff. He thought to himself, *Comic books, maybe, but just you wait and see. I'll make you proud, Dad, just you wait and see.*

His fascination had been kindled, and the first chance he had back at school that fall, he asked his teacher, "Where did the moon come from? How did it get out there circling the earth?"

The explanation he got was, "Millions of years ago the moon was floating through the solar system. As it came close, the earth's gravity reached out, pulled it into orbit, and it's been circling out there ever since." The lad sat there totally transfixed. His teacher went on, "Scientists with degrees have studied this, and that's what they say."

All the kids in his class believed it simply because their teacher said so. Even at that, as he kicked stones on the way home, he got to thinking, *My teacher really didn't answer my question—where did the moon come from in the first place?* When he got home and asked his mom about it, she said with finality, "God made it and put it right where it is; the Bible says so and that's that!" Jim's brother Chuck and he had learned at a very early age that there were two things you didn't question in their house—Mom's cooking and the Bible.

Years later, Captain Irwin pursued the "capture theory" while in advanced schooling for aeronautical engineering and quickly learned its impossibilities. In order for the moon to be captured by the earth's gravity and enter earth's orbit, it would have to travel at a relatively slow cruising speed through the solar system. At that slow speed, the sun's tremendous gravitational pull would have sucked the moon back into its fireball well before the moon ever got close to earth. That put the slam-dunk on his teacher's "capture theory," scientists with degrees or not! The reason the earth and the other planets are holding their positions in orbit around the sun and not getting sucked back in is because of their incredibly fast speed. The earth is going sixty thousand miles per hour in its swing around the sun. Like a giant yo-yo on the end of a gravitational string, the sun tugs at the earth; yet, because of the circling speed, the earth stays out there.

ஐ   ஐ   ஐ

A sudden reflex and his knee jerked up as the big thigh muscle knotted tight in a cramp. Gripping his thigh, he scrunched up against the boulder, pulled his good leg under, took a deep breath and pushed up, rasping his back against the boulder as he rose bit by bit. Stretching his knotted leg out, the painful spasm subsided; then as his head cleared, he stretched out his arms and froze. There down below, just for an instant, his eyes had caught a pinprick of light. His mind raced. Could it be the base camp? Could it be the search team? By now the summit team must have returned, and a rescue effort just might be underway. Then, dropping his arms, he shook his head. *No, don't think wistful thoughts, they wouldn't set out at night. It's far too risky; in fact, just plain dangerous.* Still, once more his eyes strained, searching for the light, but only blackness filled the abyss. Leaning slightly forward, he shifted his weight—a crack, and the ankle gave out again sending him back down, hitting the rocks with a jaw-snapping jolt. Broken teeth bit into swollen lips, and the taste of warm blood crossed his tongue.

He dropped his head to his chest and closed his eyes. For a few moments he sat slumped, arms hanging limp, one leg twisted under him. Shock, blood loss, and despair were taking their toll. Then—what was that? He cocked an ear—a low, mournful howl. Holding his breath he slowly raised his head, listening to the blackness. Again it came, this time joined by another guttural howl echoing up from the gorges below. Together they grew in intensity, culminating in a crescendo of primeval howls. "The wild dogs of Ararat," he said out loud. His eyes darted, trying to pierce the darkness.

As tension mounted in his body, he recalled the night he and his Turkish guide crouched in front of the campfire. Flames danced off the big Turk's twelve-inch dagger as he drew it out of its sheath and slid it across a whetstone, honing it razor-sharp. This tough military commando who seldom spoke seemed afraid of nothing—not the intense storms of the heights, not avalanches, not even the cutthroat bandits that roamed the foothills. Then a distant howl pierced the darkness. His gnarled hand honing the knife froze in midstroke, and just for an instant flames reflected fear crossing his eyes. Raising his dagger, he stabbed toward the black peaks above, "If the mad hounds of Ararat ever smell fresh blood . . ."

Beads of sweat broke out on the climber's forehead as fear gripped him. Clenching his fists, he put his head back against the boulder and shut his eyes tight, trying to close out the guttural howls. *Get hold of yourself. Remember, "God has not given us a spirit of fear, but of power and of love and of a sound mind." Now, use that sound mind, call upon your Creator, your personal Savior. "I will lift up my eyes to the hills—From whence comes my help? My help comes from the Lord, Who made heaven and earth."* Again he prayed, this time out loud with force, "The Lord will keep you from all harm—He will watch over your life. Even the darkness will not be dark to you; the night will shine like the day."

Tension eased as the echoing howls faded across the gorge and disappeared into the black crevasses below. Slowly he opened his bruised, swollen eyes and there, directly in front of him in all its God-created majesty, was the brilliant full moon. With purpose and strength, Colonel Irwin continued, "Then God made two great lights: the greater light to rule the day, and the lesser light to rule the night."

CHAPTER 4

As the seriously wounded climber lay slumped against the boulder, he slowly raised his head and gazed at the full moon. "*Apollo*," he whispered to the night air through swollen, bleeding lips, "the Greek word for light. How brilliant you are in the clear, crisp night air. You just don't look real from down here; and actually, you didn't become real to me until Commander Scott maneuvered out lunar lander *Falcon* into an upright position, and we got our first close-up look at your rugged mountains on our last orbit before landing." Again the injured climber focused his mind back, this time to his days as an *Apollo 15* astronaut aboard the lunar lander *Falcon*, closing on his lifetime objective—destination moon.

৪০ ৪০ ৪০

"Houston, this is absolutely incredible! We're standin' here side by side eatin' lunch and watching the greatest show on earth . . . er, 'moon.' Quick! Look there, Jim, those mountains coming up on the horizon. Here they come, hang on. Zing! They're gone! Man, I gotta tell you guys back in Houston, Jim and I feel like liftin' our feet every time we go by those."

"Roger, *Falcon*, it's a good thing the computer is doing the flying, 'cause at four thousand miles per hour, neither one of you guys could react fast enough to dodge those hills. Besides, it sounds like you sightseers are too busy gawkin' out the windows to do much else."

"Hang on there, Houston," said Commander Scott as he tapped the water bottle, sending it floating across the cabin. "*Apollo 15* is the first extended scientific mission to the moon; and in that auspicious capacity we have already made a bona fide discovery. With confidence we can categorically say the moon is not made of green cheese!" As the water bottle drifted by, Pilot Irwin grabbed it and squeezed a last swig before stowing it with the other gear in preliminary preparation for landing. Then he lightly tapped his toes, floated up, and with his mouth scooped up a couple of free-floating water globs before they could sneak behind the electrical panels and cause a short.

The cabin chatter ceased as they rounded the far side of the moon and went out of radio contact with Houston. Now, only the muffled whirring and clicking of the computers penetrated the darkened, weightless capsule. Neither man spoke as they stared out their windows, allowing themselves a brief time of reflection. As Pilot Irwin watched the huge lunar mountains rise on the horizon, hang silent for a second, then quickly disappear beneath, he thought, *Interesting how it takes so much longer to orbit the moon even though the earth is larger. The moon with its light gravity requires a much slower speed to maintain orbit than the earth with its heavier gravity.*

He chuckled to himself as he recalled the day his old high school teacher told the class, "The origin of the moon is the earth." At that, the pencil young Jim was chewing on snapped in half with a crunch. "That's right," continued his teacher. "At one time, billions of years ago, the earth was molten and hot; and as it spun at a fantastic speed, a big chunk of it flew off and went into orbit around the earth. The hole it left became the Pacific Ocean." The teacher called it the "fission" or "split-off theory."

At the dinner table that night he tossed out the new "fission theory," feeling proud of his scientific knowledge. With a clunk, his mom dropped her fork. Chuck froze with his soupspoon halfway to his mouth, all eyes shifting to Mrs. Irwin. "On the fourth day, Jim, God made the moon—out of nothing, Jim. No hunks of earth needed. Your 'split-off theory,' or whatever, doesn't work; and that's according to God's own handwriting." Chuck's eyes swung back to Jim; and with a "take that" smirk on his face, he loudly slurped his soup.

Years later, while heading up an aerospace research team, Captain Irwin discovered how right his mom was. The "split-off theory" really was "far out." The earth could never have been spinning fast enough to throw anything into space, to say nothing of a hunk as big as the moon. But assuming it did, the moon-size chunk would have gone out ten thousand miles and then shattered due to the earth's tremendous gravitational pull. But assuming it didn't shatter, it would have kept right on going straight out; that is, unless it had booster rockets on it to make it stop, turn sideways, and go into orbit around the earth. So much for the "split-off" theory.

Commander Scott poked his pilot and pointed to the countdown clock, then to their helmets. Everything became dead serious in the cabin as the enormity of what they were about to do gripped the men. In determined silence, the two astronauts pulled on their space helmets and twisted them until the seal lock snapped. It would be an extremely tricky landing—clearing several steep mountains by entering a steep trajectory while descending into a valley, crossing over three large craters, and then setting down just shy of a thousand-foot-deep canyon. As Pilot Irwin finished the final checklist, Commander Scott fired the small attitude rockets on the side of *Falcon*, maneuvering them on their backs with the big engine facing forward ready for the descent burn.

"This is it, Jim. Thirteen years of combined training all boils down to the next ten minutes." As the tension went up, the computer clock ticked down—three, two, one. The big engine burst into flame at the precise second, sending *Falcon* toward its lunar rendezvous.

Coming down to six thousand feet, the onboard computer pitched the *Falcon* nearly upright. Gray lunar mountains loomed on either side, filling the windows. Commander Scott, looking down, got his first close-up of the landing area. Pilot Irwin kept his eyes glued on the computers, calling out the numbers as they descended.

"Three thousand feet with 50 percent fuel."

A first, terse visual report: "Jim, I can't make out anything that's familiar. These mountains on either side just weren't in our simulator."

"Two thousand, 20 percent fuel."

"Houston, I don't recognize the landing zone. We've got numerous craters and boulders. It looks treacherous down there," said a tight-lipped Commander Scott.

"Roger, Commander, keep it steady. Our computer says you're right on course. How does the view outside compare with the window grid?"

"Negative, Houston. There's absolutely no matchup with the window grid, but I do see Hadley Rille."

"One thousand, 10 percent fuel." Pilot Irwin's voice was rock-steady, belying the immense inner tension.

"Wait, Jim. I think I've got something. Yeah, there they are, right below us in a perfect row—Matthew, Mark, and Luke. Houston, I've just spotted our three craters pointing to the drop zone. Yeah, there it is, and I've got the canyon now. Jimmy, we are right on the mark!"

"Two hundred feet, sixty seconds of fuel left."

"We've got boulders all over the place down there. I'm taking control and moving us over a bit." As Commander Scott switched off the computer and maneuvered the spacecraft manually, the big engine swiveled on its gimbal, shooting flame down between the twenty-foot landing pods and propelling *Falcon* sideways over the crater-marked lunar surface.

Now, locking his eyes on the precise onboard landing radar, Pilot Irwin called out, "105, 04, 03, 02, 100 feet. Thirty seconds of fuel." Lunar dust kicked up and obscured Commander Scott's vision out the windows. His hand hovered over the engine-stop button. It would be absolutely critical for him to shut down the engine at exactly ten feet—any lower and the blasting engine could kick up rocks that might rupture the thin skin of *Falcon*, destroying the pressure, the mission, and the men. Cat-whisker probes descending from the landing pods would tell them when they reached that critical ten feet. "Fifty, twenty, fifteen, ten feet—we've got a probe contact light." With fifteen seconds of fuel left, Commander Scott's hand hit the kill button.

"Bam!" shouted Pilot Irwin as the *Falcon* dropped and impacted the lunar surface. The safety cables around their waists snapped taut, keeping them from being driven to their knees. Gear jolted in the cabin. Then, absolute silence as *Falcon* pitched, hung for a second, and began to lean sideways, one of the landing pods slipping down a crater. Both men held their breath in stunned silence as *Falcon* slid toward an extremely dangerous situation. If the pitch reached forty-five degrees, there was a chance the module would tip over; then spacecraft and astronauts would become a permanent part of the moon.

Their eyes locked on the attitude indicator as the needle rose. Whispering, Pilot Irwin read the numbers, "Ten degrees and climbing—fifteen, twenty." Not a breath came from Houston. Commander Scott's hand silently moved to the blast-off button. "Twenty-one, twenty-two, twenty-three, twenty-three—we're rocking— twenty-one, twenty, twenty." Then louder, "Now we're holding steady—twenty—still steady." Then shouting, "We're holding rock firm at twenty degrees."

"Okay, Houston. The *Falcon* is on the Plain of Hadley!" radioed an exuberant Commander Scott to the world.

"Roger, *Falcon*, we show you with slight tilt to starboard, but all systems look good. You are cleared to stay."

The two astronauts turned, their eyes met; and for an instant they froze with thoughts of their families, of the hundreds of support personnel, of the astronauts who died to pave the way, of their Lord—all culminating in this one historic moment. Then, with childlike glee, they pounded each other on the back with over-sized, space-suited arms and shouted to the world, moon, and solar system, "We've done it, we've done it! Thank You, Lord, thank You!"

Back on earth, Mary Irwin's heart flooded with joy as she watched TV. Grateful tears flowed down her cheeks as she opened her Bible, hugged the children, and read the twenty-third psalm, "The Lord is my shepherd . . ."

Later, after *Falcon* was secured and the systems shut down, Pilot Irwin moved to his window, put his hands on either side, and looked at the light tan lunar surface below. As he pondered their mission, the reality of it all sunk in. They were the first extended scientific mission to the moon, and what he was looking at was real lunar soil, real rocks, real craters—he was actually on the God-created moon. He thought back to the *Apollo 8* mission, to that Christmas Eve when Commander Frank Borman, Jim Lovell, and Bill Anders emerged from the dark side of the moon for the first time and came in radio contact with earth. They took turns reading the first chapter of Genesis. "In the beginning God created . . ." That brought back a memory of his college professor's version that proclaimed, "In the beginning, stars, planets, and everything in the universe were in one mighty ball; then it exploded. The dust went out into spiral galaxies; and after billions of years, these whirlpool dust particles came together in a snowball fashion and formed stars and planets, even our own earth and moon." He called it the "big bang theory."

Raising his eyes across the undulating lunar surface toward fifteen-thousand-foot Mt. Hadley, he shook his head and thought, *If all the planets and stars of the universe had been crammed into one giant ball, it could never explode; rather, it would implode because of the incredible gravity factor, and we'd end up with a black hole. But even if it did explode, in the vacuum of space all the pieces would go straight out. Nothing would be whirlpooling or circling around anything. There is plenty of dust out here, and none of it is coming together like a snowball. It would be just like taking a handful of that fine lunar dust out there, throwing it up in the air, and watching tiny planets form—it just won't happen. And how could that so-called snowball ever come together while spinning around the earth? Shoot, there's a hundred reasons why that "big bang theory" doesn't work. All those people who made up those theories do have two things in common—first, they don't work, and second, not one of them can say where everything came from in the first place.*

"Hey, Jim, that sun's shinin' awful bright in here. You wanna put the blinders on the window so we can grab some shut-eye?" said a tuckered Commander Scott.

Putting the sunshades in place, he thought, *How different it is here—no air, no water, a very light gravity. Here the sun shines for fourteen straight days; then it's fourteen days of blackness. Let's see, we've landed on the third day of sunshine, and we'll be here for three days—that's a total of six days. That means we landed about coffee time on a lunar day, and we'll leave before lunch by lunar time, even though we've been here for three days earth time. Figure that one out,* he thought as he stripped to his long johns and snuggled into his cubbyhole sleeping quarters under the computers. After thanking the Lord for answering his prayer and the prayers of millions for a safe landing, he closed his eyes for a well-deserved, seven-hour sleep made sound by the slight lunar gravity.

A live TV camera on the side of *Falcon* transmitted the astronauts' first steps to millions of earthlings, including an exuberant Dr. Forrest, watching his set in Elmira, New York. Waving to his wife, he shouted, "Judy, come here quick! Look at this. . . . Right there, see that guy? That's Colonel Jim Irwin—remember him? He's the test pilot I operated on ten years ago out in California after that horrible plane crash. Man, just look at him hop around on the moon! That's absolutely incredible after what those smashed-up legs went through. You know, Honey, I probably won't ever walk on the moon, but at least I can say one thing—a couple of 'my legs' sure made it!"

The world watched as in the light lunar gravity, the two astronauts bounded like kangaroos to the west side of *Falcon* and prepared to get *Rover*, their lunar vehicle, into action. The entire vehicle was collapsed and folded like a double suitcase, then hinged on the side of *Falcon*. Jim pulled the kingpin and the forward half of *Rover* automatically unfolded. As it did, the front wheels popped out and locked into place, then the steering yoke came up. Dave unhinged the back half, and as it dropped, the rear wheels, communication antennas, and TV disk locked into their respective positions. Sliding straps, they lowered the suspended *Rover* to the lunar surface, then tightened the nuts and activated the batteries that powered the wheels.

"What do you think, our dune buggy gonna crank up?"

"For eight million bucks, it better. I'm not even gonna kick the tires!"

"Don't forget your seat belt," said Commander Scott as the two astronauts literally hopped in for man's first vehicle ride on the moon. Gradually picking up speed, *Rover*'s thin wire mesh tires easily traversed the lunar soil, leaving only a half-inch track as they skirted craters and popped over football-size rocks strewn across the surface on their way to the base of Mt. Hadley.

"Yee-haaa! Let's open her up."

Commander Scott pushed the yoke full forward, propelling *Rover* to its top speed—ten miles per hour. For twenty minutes they cruised the base of Mt. Hadley Delta, both men stunned by the immensity of the mountain made pristine-clear in a vision unobscured by an atmosphere. As they topped a small rise, *Rover* jolted over a large rock, hit a chuckholesize crater, and broke hard left, throwing lunar soil out as it spun up in a two-wheel skid. Both astronauts threw themselves to the top side while Dave jammed the wheels into the skid. For a second they hung on two wheels, then dropped with a soft lunar crunch to all four. They stopped. Neither man spoke as their pounding hearts subsided.

Breaking the tension, Commander Scott twisted his bulky suit around, looked back at their skid marks, and throwing his thumb back, said, "Somebody forgot to put up the 'Dip' sign back there!"

With a relieved smile Jim countered, "Yeah, they really oughta, especially on these unimproved roads. Man, we'd be sittin' here for a long time waitin' for a wrecker."

As they started back, Jim remembered the time he had posed the rollover problem to the General Motors engineers who built *Rover*. "It certainly wouldn't crush you guys since the vehicle is relatively light in the low lunar gravity. You might get caught underneath for a bit, but you'd figure something out and worm outta there."

A flight surgeon standing nearby pointed his clipboard at *Rover* and said, "The real problem would be if you should puncture your space suit on the TV antenna or some sharp object. Just a small leak and the pressure inside your space suit would quickly drop to two-and-a-half pounds. At that, you'd have about twenty seconds of useful consciousness. Then, after passing out, for all practical purposes you've had it because there's no way your buddy could manhandle you back up the ladder and stuff you into the *Falcon*. And if the hole was big enough to lose all pressure, your body parts would explode, filling the inside cavity of your space suit and helmet. And don't forget, the lunar environment is hostile; with no pressure and an outside temperature over two hundred degrees Fahrenheit, your blood would instantly boil. I suggest you don't go pokin' holes in your seven-layer suit; besides, your tailor wouldn't be one bit happy if he heard you ruined his sixty-thousand-dollar creation."

As they resumed their journey toward the canyon, Colonel Irwin thought of *faith*—faith in their life-sustaining space suits; faith in their tiny home *Falcon*; faith in the millions of components that made up their mighty rocket that blasted them away from the earth with 7,500,000 pounds of thrust; faith in Mission Control that guided and controlled their every move from 240,000 miles away; faith in the One who, according to the Bible, holds all things together—Jesus Christ.

"Hold it, Dave. Down there—see it?" Braking, Commander Scott brought *Rover* to a halt on the edge of Spur Crater. Both men peered down the drop-off. "Down there, next to that big boulder. See that baseball-size white stone kinda sittin' on that pedestal? That's exactly what the geologists want us to hunt out and pick up." Gingerly, the two men hopped and slid down the slope to the rock.

"Houston, this is incredible. I think we've met one of our objectives. Looks like somebody put it right here special for us. You can tell the geologists we've got their white rock. Now all we gotta do is get outta here without slidin' off the edge and gettin' a view of the crater from the bottom up."

Back at *Falcon*, the rest of the precision-planned day was spent carrying out exacting scientific experiments. The work was physically demanding—digging soil samples, pounding in core tubes, and setting up seismographic equipment.

At the end of seven hours, the exhausted men climbed up the ladder and crawled into *Falcon*. When the pressure gauge needle moved past the green safety line, Pilot Irwin reached over with his left hand and punched the unlock button on his right glove, twisted it to the seal-break position, and pulled it off. Tipping it over, he poured out a gloveful of sweat that slowly fell to the floor. As the men stripped to their sweat-soaked long johns, they detected a strange, acrid odor that even overpowered the perspiration smell. After some sniffing detective work, they found it came from the outside of their space suits. To their amazement they discovered that as the lunar dust that clung to their space suits came in contact with the pure cabin oxygen, it oxidized in a sort of microburn and was giving off a strong gunpowder smell. By the time they crawled into their sleeping cubbyholes, *Falcon* smelled like a cross between a Marine rifle range and the Green Bay Packers' locker room.

The work was physically demanding.

Having worked diligently throughout their three days, the astronauts managed to get just enough time to perform one last experiment prior to blast off. As millions of school kids watched on live TV back on earth, Commander Scott announced, "We shall now perform, with your help, the Galileo experiment." He moved to the side of *Falcon* and retrieved several items from the dunnage bag. "Four hundred years ago, the great scientist Galileo predicted that in the vacuum of space, objects would fall at the same speed; namely, a feather and hammer would drop and hit the ground at the same time. Now I have here in my right hand a falcon feather graciously donated by our very own mascot from the United States Air Force Academy. In my left, I hold the hammer. Watch closely as I release them at the same time. Voilà! The feather and hammer have both drifted down and hit the lunar surface at exactly the same time. We have just proved Galileo correct. Together we have made history by proving his theory, which makes it a law because we can repeat it and observe it."

*"Now I have here in my
right hand a falcon feather."*

Stepping back, the two astronauts took a last long look at their expedition site. To their right was *Rover*; to the left, *Falcon*, its gold foil reflector shining brilliantly; and directly in front, a firmly implanted flagpole bearing the American flag with outstretched stars and stripes. Then the two men knelt down and solemnly placed a small, hand-carved fallen astronaut on the lunar surface. Next to it they positioned a plaque with the names of the fourteen American astronauts and Russian cosmonauts who had given their lives in the quest of space exploration. After a moment of reverent silence and prayer, they stood; and as millions on earth watched, Colonel Irwin walked to the American flag. With the golden *Falcon* in the background, he came to attention and proudly saluted the Stars and Stripes.

Two hundred forty thousand miles back on earth, a gray-haired Father Irwin was watching his son on TV, his eyes filled with tears. As he sat on the sofa next to his wife, Elsa, he squeezed her hand and with a choking voice said, "I'm proud of you, son. Yes, sir, mighty proud."

*He came to attention and proudly
saluted the Stars and Stripes.*

&ℰ℧   &ℰ℧   &ℰ℧

Exhaustion finally overcame the wounded climber as he lay on his back staring at the night sky above Mt. Ararat. Slowly closing his battered eyes, he drifted off into blissful sleep.

CHAPTER 5

A half mile above the injured climber, the most deadly animal to man sat perched on top of a black volcanic rock. As the first golden rays of sun stabbed through the eastern peaks, the cold-blooded animal began to stir, its one-inch-long body gathering heat from the sun. The highly sensitive antennae between the fly's eyes began to twitch, searching the air for odors of decomposing or rotting material.

Far below, lying in the dark gray recess of volcanic rock, Colonel Irwin slowly opened his swollen eyes. Weakened by blood loss, dehydration, and shock, the climber was now unable to move. Still, having endured the night, he fought to keep his mind alert lest the rescuers should come and he needed to call out. His eyes struggled to follow, then fastened on the last of the full moon as it slowly descended to the western horizon, turning a deep orange in the heavy-laden desert atmosphere.

He thought, *You really never understand something and truly know it until you discover its origins, its beginning. For three days I walked your surface. I have held your very stones in my hand; the Press called the little white one the "Genesis Rock." How right they were, for Genesis means "beginning."*

He thought back to the Bible his mother had given him and her loving words, "Here, Jim, here in Genesis, the first book of the Bible, you will find the truth about where the moon, the earth, and the sun came from." Reading the Bible, he had discovered how God created all things out of nothing in six days, how God created the earth on the first day, and then, seventy-two hours later on the fourth day made the moon, the sun, and the rest of the universe.

He learned how God had created each thing with age built in; such as, on the third day, He had instantly made fully grown fruit trees with fruit on them and seeds in the fruit.

And how on the fourth day, He instantly made light that shone on the earth, having come from stars billions of light-years out in the universe. And on the sixth day, out of nothing He created Adam—a fully grown man. Tracing Adam's genealogy, he found God had made all these things less than ten thousand years ago, yet He had made each with its own specific appearance of age.

These things Colonel Irwin had accepted by faith through Christ just as Wernher von Braun, the father of America's space program, had done. Then God honored that faith by allowing man to uncover one of His basic truths about the creation of the universe and the laws that govern it. World-renowned scientists testing the "Genesis Rock" with sophisticated radiometric dating technology made one of the greatest discoveries of space exploration. They discovered that the moon and earth had come into existence at just about the same time. That simple white stone, the "Genesis Rock," found sitting on its pedestal at the base of Mt. Hadley by astronauts Scott and Irwin, had scientifically confirmed the biblical creation account.

In the quickening dawn high above, the fly's antennae became very active as they picked up the stench of an attracting odor; instantly it was airborne, searching the area down the snow ledge. The huge fly's wings beating twelve thousand times a minute droned strongly in the stillness of dawn. Hearing the distant drone that pierced the silence, the wounded climber strained his ears. *Could it be? Could it really be?* His mind raced. *That just might be a helicopter or plane. Dawn is breaking and they must have started the search and rescue by now.* Straining harder, he moved his head slightly, then pain stopped him. The distant plane-like drone started to fade. Mentally, he pleaded, *No, don't go. This way, please, this way.*

The black insect's four thousand eyes had picked up some goat droppings on the snow ledge below; it dropped quickly to them. Then the fly's antennae picked up the fresh scent of rotting blood, sending a shiver of anticipation through the now hungry insect. Instantly, the big fly was airborne, its antennae searching the air for the trail to the fresh carrion.

Once again the climber's hopes soared as he heard the droning of what he thought was surely the rescue helicopter. *It's coming closer. Come on, look down—over here, over here.* The drone grew louder and then, "Thump!" The big fly landed on the blood-caked ear. Moving quickly, it crawled into the dark inner recesses, the hairs on its six legs brushing flesh, sending a maddening sensation deep into the helpless climber's head. The animal stopped as the ear twitched in uncontrolled spasms. With a blast, it thundered out. The hungry beast circled once, then resettled on the climber's swollen upper lip, the sticky substance on its feet providing instant traction. The claws on the tip of the fly's six legs dug in as it crawled up and over the mound of swollen lip to just under the climber's nose, disappearing from his view. Pain kept him from moving even a finger. *Oh, to raise a hand and kill the beast*, he thought as his sensitive, swollen nerve ends raced wildly at the fly's clawing. A rush of air from the right unplugged nasal passage sent the fly buzzing, only to circle again and land on the bridge of his gashed nose. The petrified climber stared in horror as the beast, two inches from his eyes, began to feed on his blood.

Attracted by the smell of fresh blood wafting on the air, a second fly landed on the wounded man's throat, crawled over his Adam's apple, and began to feed. Suddenly the air was filled with the black beasts. Hundreds of them descended on the climber's face. Choking as they crawled in his nose, ears, and mouth, he rasped out, "Oh, God, is this the end?" He closed his eyes tight as the black swarm covered his face in a feeding frenzy.

"Jim . . . Jim! Colonel Irwin-n-n-n . . ." The hail rose, then faded as the rescuer swung in a calling circle, hands cupped to mouth.

"Jim, it's Monte—if you hear me, call out." This time the call was louder, as the searcher shouted directly at the unseen climber lying in the crevasse barely a hundred feet uphill.

"I'm here, I'm here." His weak voice didn't even raise the flies. *I've got to call out. Lord, help!* Choking, with a cough he cleared his blood-clotted throat and rasped out loud, "Here, over here."

The searcher started to turn down the slope; then he stopped stone-still, cocking his head. A slight breeze blowing downhill toward him carried a whisper from the rocks above, "Here, Monte, over here."

Standing ramrod straight, he yelled, "Jim, I think I heard you. Call again, Gimme a call, Jim."

With all the force the wounded climber could muster, he rasped, "Over here, brother, over here."

Swinging his head and shoulders around directly toward the call for help, the rescuer spotted a hand and arm draped over the black rocks. "Jim, Jim, I've got you sighted." Then cupping hands to mouth, he let go a bellow heard clear across the gorge, "It's him, I've got him!" Quickly he pulled a smoke bomb from his jacket, detonating it to alert the rest of the team. Looking up, he charged the hill.

As the rescuer clawed and crashed over rocks in his dash up the steep slope toward the wounded climber, the cloud of flies lifted, then blew off in the quickening cool breeze. Colonel Irwin slowly opened his swollen, bloodshot eyes. Gradually, white snow-capped peaks, framed by pure blue sky came into focus. For a moment he drank in the majestic sight, letting it sink deep into his heart. Then, with tears of thanks streaming down his bloodstained face, he said, "I will lift up my eyes to the hills—From whence comes my help? My help comes from the Lord, Who made heaven and earth."

EPILOGUE

Colonel James B. Irwin graduated from the Naval Academy at Annapolis in 1951 with a bachelor of science degree. He earned a master of science degree from the University of Michigan in 1957; and honorary doctorates have been conferred on him from Samford University, William Jewell College, and the University of Michigan. After graduation from the Naval Academy, he was commissioned as an officer in the United States Air Force, becoming a test pilot and missile project officer at Air Defense Command. Upon being accepted as an astronaut in the Apollo program, he spent five years in intensive study for the first extended scientific expedition to the moon—*Apollo 15*. Among his many awards, he received the NASA Distinguished

Service Medal, the Air Force Distinguished
Service Medal, the United Nations Peace
Medal, the Robert J. Collier Trophy, the
George Washington Medal for the Freedoms
Foundation, and the Churchman of the Year
Award.

Colonel Irwin founded High Flight Foundation, an evangelistic outreach based in Colorado
Springs, Colorado. Before his sudden death in
1991, he and his wife Mary traveled much of
the world, giving his testimony of a personal
Creator God to millions.

ABOUT THE AUTHOR

P aul Thomsen graduated from the University of Wisconsin (Madison) in 1960. Through his career as an international executive and corporate owner, he has lived in and traveled much of the world.

Paul and his wife, Julie, have created Dynamic Genesis, Inc., and endeavor to produce books for the Creation Adventure Series, of which *Flight of the Falcon* is a part. They also conduct seminars for school students, teaching them how to answer questions on origins the way the public school textbooks present them, and then "qualify" their answers with a nongradable, biblical, scientific answer. This "qualifier" system has received enthusiastic approval from both teachers and students.

The Thomsens have seven children and live on a small lake in northern Wisconsin.

While in the San Diego area, visit the

Institute for Creation Research

and its *exciting*

Museum of Creation and Earth History

10946 Woodside Avenue North
Santee, California 92071
or call for information at (619) 448-0900